THE HAUNTING OF
MOON[...]

JEFF MARTINEZ

authorHOUSE®

AuthorHouse™
1663 Liberty Drive
Bloomington, IN 47403
www.authorhouse.com
Phone: 1-800-839-8640

First published by AuthorHouse   11/22/2011

ISBN: 978-1-4670-6711-9 (sc)
ISBN: 978-1-4670-6710-2 (ebk)

Printed in the United States of America

Any people depicted in stock imagery provided by Thinkstock are models,
and such images are being used for illustrative purposes only.
Certain stock imagery © Thinkstock.

This book is printed on acid-free paper.

THE HAUNTING OF
MOON ISLAND

Contents

CHAPTER I

THE RISE AND FALL OF
MOONSCAR

I remember going every summer with my little sister Lula to New Orleans, the true Paris of the West. I was just a small kid. One of the memories of that wonderful city that really sticks out for me would have to be all of my Grandpa's stories he would spin for us. There were all these exciting tales of ghosts and pirates.

One of the stories that he'd often told us directly relates to the tale I'm about to share with you. It's about an old scallywag, a pirate named Jack Villar: the vicious Captain Moonscar!

• • • •

Now, dear old Moonscar started out as an ordinary merchant sailor. He sailed on a large red ship called the *Sea Maiden*.

But as good stories of rollicking pirates go, the *Sea Maiden* was attacked by a group of brutal scurvy dogs! Not wanting to go down without a fight, Villar fought hard and well. Even then, the vicious pirates who had attacked his ship and crew were too bloodthirsty, too quick with their blades. One of the pirates even slashed the poor seaman's face giving him a nasty scar shaped like a crescent moon.

It was a battle to the last man standing, and Villar was the last man. Well, at least from his merchant crew. And having respect for the pirate crew, (though really due to the massacre of his own crew) Villar had requested passage upon the *Lady Doom*. Seeing how gallantly and forcefully he fought them, they were more than happy to oblige his request and have him on board. They always could use a fighter like Jack Villar.

His first attempts at piracy were, to say the least, not at all frightening, not even slightly threatening. The only hint of threat had come more so from his new "Moonscar" nickname and the scar from which the name-sake came rather than his supposed presence. His piracy skills were based more so on negotiation and

• • • •

conning rather than actual brutality of most pirates. Still, over time the title of Captain had been passed down to him.

But as even more time had passed on, and the fear he had struck into the hearts had completely diminished, his bloodthirsty crew had a stronger desire for mutiny!

Is it ever a good idea to wheel-and-deal as a pirate? Oh, indeed it is! Be as that may, the more you use basic bargaining skills the more likely you are to lose your potency as a threat. As a motley crew of murderers and thieves, being taken seriously is everything!

So to prove the he had as much guts as the next pirate, he vowed that the next captain to turn him down would unwittingly be signing a death wish for him and his crew. Moonscar and his crew had made a horrible massacre of the poor crew that had refused his offer taking whatever they could get their greedy little hands upon. As it was with that offer, any forthcoming offer he made that would be refused, would mean one hell of a bloody mess for those who had refused. Due to the new threat that he had brought to the Caribbean the refusals became less and less frequent.

Still Jack Villar had become weary of all the paranoia that had come from being the dreaded Captain

• • • •

Moonscar. Authorities from every nation with colonies in the Caribbean were in want of his head. It had become time for the old seadog to retire a rich man.

So due to his clever ruthlessness, he had devised an evil plan to rid himself of all of his crew and to keep the rich stuff all to his own greedy hands.

He had brought them to a deserted pirate island and he killed each and every last one of them. He had heard a rumor that another pirate crew was following them so they had buried the treasure for a few days.

What he hadn't expected was that the crew was a part of the Spanish navy ready to massacre the pirate crew. Being the only survivor of a mutiny, they took them aboard their ship as a prisoner. Poor Captain Moonscar was unable to make a bargain of any kind with the Spaniards. Due to Moonscar's own greed, he had become royally screwed.

What happened to him after they had made port? Nobody knows for certain. Some say he was hanged. Others say he never survived the journey back. And curious souls speculate that he had ended up in New Orleans taking the name De Chagney . . .

• • • •

In my humble opinion, I would to think that Moonscar retired a nice humble life. But in all honesty that's just hopeful thinking. The likelihood of that happening is so slim that it's not really even worth mentioning.

CHAPTER II

THE CHARTS

I t felt so very strange coming all the way back to New Orleans after so many years. You see, the little old shack in the murky swamps we were staying at during our summer trips down there was actually located at a camping ground. It was just outside the city limits. Swamps and bayous are just perfect for that. Especially with Grandpa's banjo playing.

He actually lived on a cotton plantation. A plantation is a big house where cotton is grown. He wasn't the owner or anything as grand as that, but he was living in the servant quarters working for the owners. It was a decent living with good people all around even if he didn't own a home himself.

• • • •

Now Lola and I had returned to New Orleans for a simple reason: our grandfather had croaked. Neither I nor Lula has seen him in years so we were a little detached from him. Sending letters to each other once a year doesn't really count.

Of course, our dear old mother would slap us but good though for being so damn blunt about the topic. He was our blood after all, and we did know that he had loved us.

It was especially strange talking with the current owners of the estate. It seemed like they couldn't really care less whether or not Grandpa had lived or not. If you ask me that's taking detachment to a whole new nasty level. Even then, as detached as they were the Deverauxs were actually very cordial with me and my sister.

Their names were Jean and Marie Deveraux. They were nice enough with us, just a bit stiff in manner.

They were both short and pretty stout in their build. They were quite young surprisingly. They lived on this small antebellum mansion, no bigger than three stories tall. Despite the small size there was an unsettling quality about it.

They spoke their southern United States dialect of French beautifully.

• • • •

"Your grandfather was a good man, Mon Ami," Jean had been telling us. "But we were planning on moving away from this place anyway. It just became too much trouble keeping up an estate like this with just the three of us living here."

Lula was extremely curious as to why they were acting so detached to someone that they were presumably fond of. With that being said, she done flat out asked them. "Sounds like you dug him. So why are you so cold towards him now?"

After she had finished asking her question, Marie had stared at her. I was so embarrassed I could have wet myself. Marie lit herself a clove and looked Lula straight in the eye. "The answer is simple, Cher. We are in New Orleans. This is still the dirty old south of them old days. The issues of class that were so prominent during the Civil War are still strong today.

They are just better hidden."

The couple was essentially one of them image-over-substance type people that you always see in those fashion shows. That is always a disappointing discovery. It was easy for me to see all of the fury that Lula was trying to avoid. Luckily she was able to conceal it pretty well and enjoy the couple.

• • • •

Anyway, let's get back to the story at hand and how it relates to the fearsome Captain Moonscar. So as the legend goes, when he was on that Spanish Naval vessel, he had made a few navigational charts. These charts were said to have a route to the island where Moonscar had massacred his own crew, an island which had come to be known as *Pirate Island.*

Once the Deverauxs had escorted us to Grandpa's room in the servant quarters, they told us to feel free and have a look around. Since Lula and I were such a curious duo we were rather liberal with how we would interpret the invitation.

We had pretty much taken the place apart. We ransacked that room good. It was a good thing we did because behind on old mirror was a secret compartment. In that compartment so cleverly hidden (yeah, right) we found some navigational charts which seemed to have been from the 1700s. Perhaps these charts were of a valuable nature. We could get some decent money . . . Or maybe they were the long lost charts of Captain Moonscar himself!

We immediately found the Deveraux couple and asked them if we could use the charts. Jean looked them over rather quickly then turned to me. "You know what Jack? Keep them. We have no use for those charts."

● ● ● ●

My eyes bugged out like Marty Feldman's! Was he really that serious? "Surely you gotta be joking with me here. Just take them? Like that?" I tried to confirm with Jean.

Jean? He just shrugged his shoulders with no interest in the topic whatsoever. "The sea had never interested me, and neither did pirate treasure. Besides I'm too busy for adventures if those charts lead up to any adventure."

"Oh, trust me Mes Amis. Much too busy," remarked Marie.

We shook their hands hard and left running! These charts could really lead to something. Maybe they were of some historical importance. Maybe they really were the navigational charts to Pirate Island! Either way as we drove back to the hotel we knew one thing, this once going to be very exciting!

CHAPTER III

MATTER OF AUTHENTICITY

A s soon as we left the Deveraux estate and got into the downtown area Lula and I stopped to eat at a whole-in-the-wall establishment specializing in good old southern fried chicken. And let me tell you something. It was the best goddamned fried chicken that I ever in my short little life had. "Popeye's" doesn't have anything on this place. Of course it doesn't have anything on "Kentucky Fried Chicken" either so that's a bad contrast if you ask me.

Of course, Lula wasn't at all impressed with the delicacy I was thoroughly enjoying. I think that she was just too excited about those navigational charts we found, dreaming of rich stuff in the Caribbean. She just couldn't keep her mouth shut about them once we

● ● ● ●

left the estate. "Jack! Do you know what this means?" she asked me with uncharacteristic enthusiasm. She's usually so negative.

"I assume that you're going to tell me," I replied before I took a big old chunk of fried chicken from my yummy leg.

"It means that you and I can sell it to a museum for a really hefty fee, Jack! It means in a word 'money'!" She done nearly jumped out of her seat as she was explaining it to me.

After I had swallowed up the big old chunk of fried chicken I looked up at her and smiled. "It's true. Those charts may very well have some historical significance. But," I said wanting her to shake with anxious curiosity. "There is also the off-chance that those may be the very charts to Pirate Island that Moonscar had drawn."

Her eyes had opened up wide to my little suggestion. She seemed to be very pleased with it. However, what I had said after had crushed her desire if only for a little bit.

"Then again, the most likely scenario is that they are useless fakes," I said lighting up a cigarette.

"Why do you always have to shatter my dreams?" she retorted.

• • • •

"Because it's fun," I explained in a playfully teasing manner.

After checking into our hotel, we immediately searched through a phonebook and looked up the archeology department at New Orleans Sate College. We told the dean what we had and they were more than happy to have it analyzed for us, but that it wouldn't be ready for a few days.

That was perfect for us. The following day we needed to be back at the Deveraux estate to pack up Grandpa's belongings. For the couple of days following, we were able to enjoy the wonderful city. We went all over the place from hoodoo shops to jazz joints but that was an adventure in and of its self. Let's get back to them charts.

Lula and I went to the college's archeology de-partment and asked for a Pr. Hickory Black. He saw us immediately and welcomed us into his office. He was a tall man with slicked back hair and a decent everyday suit. He talked in a basic southern draw, slow and articulate.

"Well, thank you for coming Mr. Olsen," he said with a warm smile. "I have some information about those navigational charts you had sent to my department."

• • • •

"It's not too disappointing I hope," I said shaking his hand. Lula politely waved. "Although I can't say I'm not expecting anything."

"Actually," he said with a mischievous gleam in his eye. "I think that you would like it. Tell me what you know about Jack Villar."

My eyes bulged like they did when the Deveraux couple had given us the charts. "You mean Moonscar?"

Were these really the long lost charts to the most notorious island in the Caribbean? "Are those the charts to Moon Island?"

As I said that Lula was jumping around his office she was so full of raw excitement. Wow. She has been pretty exuberant during this story. Usually she is very confrontational and monotone.

"As a matter of fact," he replied, "They are."

"How sure are you?" I asked.

"I have double checked numerous times, Mr. Olsen," he notified me. "I can assure you as a scientist that this is in fact the real thing. I have even received a letter of confirmation from my superiors. Where did you manage to stumble across them?"

"Deveraux Manor," I said emotionally aroused by the idea of finding pirate treasure.

• • • •

Pr. Black pondered over what I just told him and smiled. "That would be the place one might be privy to find them if they cared to look. It's said to be haunted," he said.

"Let's go," I said. "Let's make the voyage to Moon Island."

Lula looked at me almost blankly. Then she wrapped her arms around me squeezed me so tight that it was giving my lungs slight difficulty. "Thank you! You are the best brother in the world!" She practically screamed that comment. But I loved hearing her appreciation.

"Can a rusty old school professor tag along with you all?" asked Dr. Black.

"Welcome aboard," I said.

"That's good, because I have already taken the liberty of looking for a ship."

"Did you find one?" I asked.

No," said the Professor. "Nobody seemed to be interested."

I couldn't let that slide. I had to give him a 'that won't cut it' look.

Our next stop was Lafitte's Landing . . .

Chapter Iv

LAFITTE'S LANDING

N ow, Lafitte's Landing is an old wharf right off the coast of the city. It was named after the infamous Jean Lafitte, a privateer for the French government. A Privateer is a seaman who is commissioned by a country to harass enemy ships.

As we walked along the harbor I took a nice whiff of the salty sea air. It reminded me of all those pirate movies I always used to rent as a kid; *Black Swan*, *the Goonies* and *Treasure Island*. Lula always teased me about my desire to become a pirate. Well, she wasn't laughing any more.

The harbor had a few grottos and taverns across the pathway. I was enjoying all of the pirate shops it had. I felt like a tourist. I ended up buying a few books on the subject. As I read them on the voyage down to Pirate Island I was a little surprised (and disappointed) that none gave any mention to Moonscar.

But let's get back to my yarn. We asked around for a decent tavern to find a crew and whoever we asked kept bringing up Admiral Benbow. So of course, that's where we stopped. It was dark and misty. The smell of cigarettes and alcohol filled the place up. At first, Lula and I were a bit taken back by it. Then we remembered those cantinas we paid a visit to in Tijuana, Mexico. This place seemed somewhat tame.

We took a seat at the bar and ordered a couple of beers. We started talking to the bartender about an archeological voyage to Isla Tesoro; a deserted island that used to hold a Spanish fort in the Caribbean. As I mentioned the Caribbean all eyes in the tavern turned towards me with great interest. But of course, not everybody would be happy to hear our suggestion. One such sailor was questioning our motives.

"Isla Tesoro? There isn't anything on that island except that damn tourist crap," the sailor retorted.

I smiled politely at him and said that he would be very surprised at how much is left on that island and I turned back to the bartender. But that didn't sit too

•   •   •   •

well with the antagonistic sailor. "And I say you're just full of crap!"

"That very well may be what you think but it's none of your business either way," I told coolly. "With that being said if you get out of our face like I know you're going to I might convince my sister to forgive a simple mistake like that."

The sailor and I stared at each other for what seemed like an eternity. Finally he took a forceful swing for my face. I blocked the punched and kicked him in the gut. I jumped on a table and flicked open a switchblade knife from my back pocket.

Now, all the eyes in the Admiral Benbow were watching the fight with an intense interest. Even though New Orleans is a big city, I doubt that barroom brawls are as common as I thought.

After busting open a Budweiser bottle, the sailor jumped onto the table also. He tried thrusting the bottle neck at me but he was just too slow. Thrusting for his shoulder I get a shallow stab in and kicked the beer bottle out of his hand. I slugged him in his face knocking him out.

There were a few moments of silence . . . really awkward silence. Once the silence had passed the bar patrons went back to their good friend Evan and mindless chit-chat.

Lula was awed by what she had just witnessed. "Why and how did you just do that?" she asked me.

"I know. I was being reckless," I told her rather nonchalantly. "That man was picking a fight with me though." I think I was trying to justify my actions to myself rather than her.

"But that was just amazing, Jack! Whoever knew that your teenage street fights would ever come in handy?" She was actually being quite serious. Usually I can sense a bit of sarcasm. Not this time.

"Bet you can manage yourself in a fight," said the bartender pretending be iffy about my skills.

"Well," I said, "Where my sister and I are planning on going some fighting experience is a pretty good idea. As I said, it's an island in the Caribbean. We are just completely clueless about what to expect."

"Well, what's the name of the island again?" he asked. "I didn't catch it."

Lula was certainly ready to answer but before she could I cupped her mouth and smiled apologetically at him. Lula never catches on when I give false information.

●　　●　　●　　●

"It's called Isla Tesoro," I told the bartender passively. If I were to actually speak the name of the island, eyes too greedy for the job would hear. I wanted good honest people. At least as good and honest as possible considering the place we were looking for a crew. I'm realistic. "Do you know any crew who would be the least bit interested in good honest work?"

I lit myself up one of my "Morley's" as he pondered the question for a moment or two. He turned his head to his right. "You see that feller with the jean jacket down yonder?" I followed his gaze and spotted the rough looking man. "He may look like a crook but he ain't."

I thanked the bartender and walked over to the gentleman. Under his tattered denim jacket was a black jolly roger t-shirt. I believe it was Calico Jack's skull and crossed swords. It really looked like he needed a decent shave. "The bartender told me that you were an honest sailor. I want to hear from your own mouth how true that is."

He bashfully grinned a bit as he spoke his piece. "Ah, he's just being generous. I try my damnedest to live an honest but I ain't perfect."

That was the best answer possible.

• • • •

I took a drag of my cigarette and I leaned forward to the sailor. "I may have some work for you. There's a decent payoff. You game?" I purposed.

He asked for more some more information and I gave him as much as I possibly could without giving too much away.

"And I suppose that you would like to come along to," he pondered.

"Along with that archeologist and my dear sister Lula," I confirmed.

Rubbing his rough beard he smiled at the idea. And he held out his hand. I grabbed a hold of it and shook it like crazy. "Jack Olsen, Sir. Thank you very much!" I told him. I may have been a bit too enthusiastic.

"Eddie Rackham. Welcome aboard the Sea Angel," he said with just as much enthusiasm.

CHAPTER V

THE VOYAGE

The voyage for the most part was pretty uneventful. Being a part of the paycheck made it easy for Lula and me not to do as much of the hard labor. Although if we were needed, we were more than happy to oblige.

My favorite duty onboard the *Sea Angel* was cooking duties in the galley. The official cook Mrs. Rackham made the best jambalaya in the Gulf of Mexico. Damn good tea also.

Even then, there is one screwy incident that I feel is relevant to this little novella at hand . . .

It took place during dinner one evening. I had just helped Mrs. Rackham set up the table for some bourbon chicken and some mashed potatoes. In came Lula along with Pr. Black and Eddie Rackham and his first mate Johnson. His first name was never told to us.

Everybody was complimenting Mrs. Rackham and me about the delicious Cajun food that we had whipped together for us.

Now, Rackham was a sailor. He would definitely know how to get to Isla Tesoro. As it turns out, Isla Tesoro is in the same general area as Pirate Island. That being the case, it was easy to fool Rackham and Johnson. Whether that was the right thing to do from the very start my doubts grow stronger as time passes on, but what's done is done.

I lit myself a cigarette to go with the peach iced tea that Mrs. Rackham and I had made. I was quite surprised to find out that neither Rackham nor Johnson smoked. Having a little drink of course was a totally different story.

Pr. Black did enjoy the occasional cigar which made us more comfortable about our cancer sticks onboard.

Out of nowhere, Pr. Black had jumped for joy while Lula and I had no clue as to why he was doing so, just that he was excited about our voyage for some reason. Rackham had finally asked him why and then it happened, the slip up . . . "Why we ain't going to Isla Tesoro. We're going to Moon Island of course." Just as

• • • •

he said that, a terrible guilt came over him. He knew damn well what he had done.

Rackham's eyes widened partly with amazement and partly at the hurt of withholding information. "We're going to Pirate Island you say?"

I took a drag of my Morley's cigarette and I nodded at him in confirmation. I then looked down in my guilt shame. I hesitated before speaking as I wished to express myself respectfully yet honestly. "I was unfamiliar with your work in New Orleans. I wanted to learn more about your character before giving you the information. It was an extra security measure. Is that understandable?" He nodded his head and excused himself from the table.

Once he left, I pulled Pr. Black aside. I looked him straight in the eye. I said to him. "Don't you ever do something that careless on my voyage."

"I'm the expert here," he retorted. "Not you!"

"And I'm the guy who's paying you," I said coolly taking a drag of my cigarette as he stormed out of the galley.

CHAPTER VI

THE ARRIVAL

That following morning we finally saw some land . . . at least on the scanner. The fog was so thick that far sight was heavily impaired. I felt like it was a going to be a ghost story. As it turns out, this is a ghost story. I lit a cigarette as we hovered around Rackham while he checked the scanner.

"Are you sure this is the right island?" I asked Rackham. He nodded. Lula was getting scared as she watched the fog surround the outside of the boat. She knew something was up.

Luckily we made port where there was already a harbor. After all, the island had been previously occupied by pirates and buccaneers over 250 years ago.

• • • •

Still, with the fog surrounding the island, it was hard to make heads or tails of the situation at hand.

Rackham, Johnson and I stepped out onto the dock while Lula and the others stayed onboard for a brief period.

As we walked down the dock we saw this cave tattered really badly. It was used by the pirates as a hideout presumably. I lit myself a cigarette as I looked up. Right above the entrance to the cave was a carved out skull and crossed swords. I could have sworn that thing was blinking, staring right at me. As I asked the other guys with me what they thought about the carving they both felt a hint of doom coming along to join them.

We immediately went back onboard to the others. It seemed like a good idea to bring them into the cave along with us, for there is safety in numbers.

As we got to the threshold of the cave, we realized something that made us feel pretty damn stupid; it was the beginning of some river. And the river boat was back at the *Sea Angel*. Damn. We walked all the way back to the cave for nothing. I waited near the entrance with Mrs. Rackham and Lula while the other three went to get it.

• • • •

I looked up at that carved-out Jolly Roger on the entrance and I could swear he was chuckling at our misfortune. Maybe Moon Island really was haunted. If so, that Jolly Roger was being a real jerk.

The three of us just sat on the rocks, not uttering a single word. There was just no reason to. Finally, I brought up the Jolly Roger to them. "Whoever carved it out has a real knack for detail," I said.

Mrs. Rackham just stared at the thing blankly while Lula was going crazy for it. She liked skulls and such, perhaps a bit too much for a proper young lady. This was no exception. I am certain that if she could take it home with her, she would have.

"It is the very essence of divine decadence," admired Lula. "Any self-respecting eccentric would love to have that in their home."

"I don't like it none," Mrs. Rackham said. She seemed to also sense that something seemed a bit off. "I could swear that damned death head keeps grinning at me."

My expression had become gloomier upon hearing this comment from her. This was when I first learned the lesson of never taking ghost legends for granted. You never know if the legends just happen to be fact. "Yeah, I felt the same thing, Mrs. Rackham."

• • • •

Finally the other three adventurers showed up. Rackham still could not look straight at the Jolly Roger. Now I figured Eddie Rackham as tough guy, strong in body ands spirit. Now if that tough guy is looking at a piece of stone in fear then you know for sure that there's something rotten on Pirate Island.

"I don't want to take any chances. I want everybody to be on their guard," I ordered. "I'm not sure I believe in ghosts but I do know that it's better to be safe than sorry." I lit up a cigarette as everybody nodded in agreement. "Are you guys ready to seek some salty old pirates?"

Everybody smiled as we boarded that little boat. I took a drag of my cigarette as Rackham started rowing. Pr. Black turned on his flashlight. It was so huge that it reminded me of the flashlights that Mulder and Scully carried around in *The X Files*.

I was smiling a devilish smile as we moved forward into the cave. This was it! I finally made it to Moon Island! You would be so proud, Grandpa.

The flashlight then caught sight at something very strange. It was a skeleton at a helm. To makes things sinister he had knifes sticking out his eyes. In all of the legends I've heard about the Island, I have never known any ships to crash. Even then, how the hell did

• • • •

this little vignette end up so perfectly in tact? This was something I had to check out.

"Head for the corpse at the helm," I told Rackham, He did so, and I stepped off. I took my flashlight and scoped for some ideas for why this seemed so perfect. Finally, I spotted it. A piece of parchment was stick-ing out his chest. I opened it up and read what it had to say. "Los piratas son advertidos." Pirates, be warned.

This stiff was murdered. What wasn't clear is whether it was a deed of ruthless pirate captain or a Spanish naval officer. Either way, there was no doubt that we were on the right track. And we were going to keep moving forward.

I hopped back on the boat. "What was it?" Pr. Black asked.

"It was a warning against pirates," I informed everybody. "The man was murdered."

"Who left it?" asked Johnson.

"I have no clue," I replied. At the time I really didn't have a clue. But I was hell-bent on finding out who did.

With each little murder trap that we saw, the sicker everybody got. Even Lula who usually loves gruesome stuff felt uncomfortable. "This island is cursed. I can feel in my bones," lamented Johnson. "Being raised in

● ● ● ●

New Orleans don't help none either." New Orleans is a place where the spirit world is said to come alive.

Pr. Black retorted in a patronizing way. "Well, I didn't know that you believe in fairy tales Mr. Johnson. I guess you believe in Santa Claus to." He was cracking himself up as he said this. But he was the only one.

Johnson just looked down into the dark water in a brooding manner. "Jack is right. Better safe than sorry."

To help the poor guy out I got my two cents into the conversation. "You never know, Professor. Fate has a funny way making people eat their words."

As decent as he seemed when we first met, everybody liked the Professor less and less.

"Only in ways that exist, Mr. Olsen.," he told me. "Not fantastical ways."

We finally saw some daylight at the end off the tunnel but the way the water was moving, it was clear that we were headed for a waterfall. "Everybody, hold on tight to the boat."

"Why?" Mrs. Rackham asked.

"It's a waterfall. There's telling no how far down it is," Rackham told his wife. "Best listen to Mr. Olsen on this."

• • • •

I knew this was really going to put a knot in my stomach but that just thrilled me even more as it did Lula. Those were always our favorite kinds of rides in amusement parks.

However, the rest of our crew wasn't as accepting of the situation, and rightfully so. There was no way to know how far it was until we got to the bottom of the fall, or if we would even survive. I turned to the others and they all had a look of impending doom as if death was right around the corner.

"Well, here we go," I told everybody a bit unsure myself of what was really ahead of us. To say that I wasn't scared would be a big mistake. I'm just better at hiding my fears then most people.

CHAPTER VII

THE PIRATE TOWN

We finally made it to the edge and down we went! The speed was unlike anything that I have ever felt before! Damn straight my stomach turned as we went down, our hair blowing in the wind! Mrs. Rackham was screaming bloody murder! It must have been a good 5 story drop into the huge pond below us. Luckily, the pond was about 25 feet deep making the land less risky.

But what lay before us was the most incredible place that I have ever been to. It was a colonial town, the likes of which has never been seen as it originally was for over 200 years. Sure you can find them all over the east coast but not without all the modern shops and

● ● ● ●

what not. But this? This was the real deal! The genuine article! I was ecstatic!

"This place is beautiful!" shouted Lula as she scoped out the town in the distance.

"Let's get to land right away to scope the town out." I suggested and everybody started rowing as fast, as hard as they possibly could. And we made it to the town. "Alright, explorers. Let's go exploring!" I shouted with all the joy that I was feeling!

Everybody went their separate ways as I stood there wide-eyed in amazement. The historical significance of this find would guarantee that none of us will be hurting financially after this. I've got to admit that this did make me feel a bit like Indiana Jones.

I went to grab a cigarette from my shirt but I just remembered. I wet them coming down the water fall. So I slowly walked around the place in amazement and then my crew was staring at me as if they no longer cared about the beauty that this pirate town had . . . as if they were scared of something. I pulled out my switchblade cautiously and flicked it open. I would have pulled out my Beretta but that was just as wet as my cigs. I walked slowly to the town square and then I saw what they had just seen. I almost wish that I hadn't seen it though.

● ● ● ●

Somehow, there was a message just for me and my crew. I don't see how it couldn't be for us because it was written in fresh blood. It was right outside a tavern called *Seaman's Grotto* where they always used to have signs hanging right outside the door. STAY AWAY.

I scoped out the surrounding area spotting an old man dressed in a tattered Georgian outfit about ten feet away. It was clear that this guy was giving me an evil wink. So I ran towards him and tackled him down. The wink was replaced by fear. "Who the hell are you?"

I shouted in his face.

He started laughing. "Ye came looking some pirate treasure, I'm sure. I'm the man who will make damn certain that you'll fail at that," the old man taunted. "Because none of you deserve what treasure this deathly place has."

"What gives you the right to play God?" I retorted.

"What gives you the right to take the treasure from this town?" he asked smiling at me, taunting me. That bastard was really getting into my head.

Well, from that last statement I introduced my fists to his face bloodying him up real good. Once I pounded on him for a few seconds I asked the man again, "Who the hell are you?"

•   •   •   •

"My name is Israel Adams, a sailor under Jack Moonscar," he informed me. Once he did so, I slowly got up from my violent position and moved away as I came to the eerie conclusion that Pirate Island was indeed haunted by the ghosts of dead pirates. My suspicions were to my mind confirmed as I turned back to where old Israel was only to find that he was longer there. And I couldn't call the Ghostbusters either.

CHAPTER VIII

HOW TO PROCEED

I walked back over to my group and I sat down on a rock between Lula and Rackham. I stared out into the distance unable to go further at that moment. What the hell was this place? How did it get cursed? How does that affect my team? That meeting with Israel Adams was raising so many damned questions. How could I proceed any farther?

"Well?" asked Lola expecting some grand revelation around this tricky situation that we've just got our selves into.

"Well what?" I snapped. This wasn't just one of Grandpa's stories anymore. "This isn't some spooky tale to frighten us in the bayous."

● ● ● ●

"But what the hell does that matter? You're Jack Olsen!" she questioned.

"What makes me different than any other man?"

"The fact that you have enough balls to go through this stuff. All the other bastards I know would have pissed their pants and run at the first sign of trouble," she explained to. The sad thing is it's true. "But not you Jackie Boy, not you. You take a drag of your cancer stick and you tell us to take precautions."

"Frankly, it's just blood. What's the big fuss about it?" questioned Rackham.

His wife looked at him shocked at his comment. "The blood was fresh. There is something evil on this island."

"What does it matter if it's fresh?" asked the Professor. "We came here to do a job so let's do the job."

The heat radiating from the sun was so strong on that island that my cigarettes had dried up rather quickly. Well, quickly enough. I lit one up and took a nice long drag while I contemplated the idea.

"Well," I figured, "If we back down now then this entire trip would have been a complete waste of time. And I would rather not waste anybody's time, especially something that cold make you or break you guys."

• • • •

"But this place is dangerous," snapped Johnson. "We're only going to get ourselves killed of we decide to stick around."

"The souls are getting restless, restless and angry," warned Mrs. Rackham. "They're fixing to kill us all I reckon. I would rather be safe than sorry, Mr. Olsen."

"Well, we can figure out some ways to take some safety precautions without leaving, Mrs. Rackham," I explained to her.

"Besides, the historical significance of this find is absolutely amazing," informed Lula. "It's worth the risk staying."

"Well, I'm not leaving until I got some of that treasure," snapped the Professor. I started chuckling at the chubby old man.

"You're putting your foot down, aren't you Pr. Black? Does it make you feel like a big strong man?" I taunted. There was something that was just a bit off that I couldn't quite put my finger on. Of course, now it was becoming crystal clear. He was just another greedy old man. Since I was too lazy to deal with his pissy mood I gave him this one. "I'll go along with your greed, Pr. Black. Under one condition; just as long as we do things my way."

"You better be willing to go along with it," smiled Pr. Black. He looked as if he had won the world heavyweight championship from Mike Tyson. The poor idiot had the foolish idea that he had me beat and broken. The only thing was that I had a thing or two up my sleeve.

As Lula was jumping up and down for joy and hugging so incredibly tight that I could barely breathe I had motioned her to the side. She was as curious as she was concerned. "What's wrong, Jack?" she asked me.

"Now you just watch out for the Professor, Lula. He's a shady character," I warned her. I was trying to be as warm and loving as I possibly could.

"Yeah, okay Jackie Boy. Whatever you say," she reassured me. I gave her slight smile and little hug. I patted her on the back and took a drag of my cigarette.

As Lula and I headed back to the group, Rackham and Johnson were scoping out the mountain we entered the pirate town from to see if there was another way up. Mrs. Rackham was busy making some poor boy sandwiches for everybody. On a side note, let me say that those were some delicious poor boys. Thank you Mrs. Rackham.

Now, let's get down to business. I immediately turned to Rackham and Johnson. "Is there any other

● ● ● ●

way up?" They nodded. "What about with the river boat?" I asked.

"Well, if we have three people I'm sure it can be done," answered Rackham.

"I want you, Johnson and Pr. Black to go back up and get whatever we may need for three nights," I ordered. "Are you guys good with that?" They all nodded. "Once you get back, I want you to meet us inside Seaman's Grotto. That'll be where we'll stay."

"But that's where we saw the bloody sign," said Mrs. Rackham with a bit of fear in her voice.

"That's why we're going to be extra careful while we're in there," I told her. "Of course, we do have the other option of staying out here on this lovely haunted tropical island with all of the tropical insects and snakes."

Once I said that, both of the ladies and Johnson quickly decided to go down to the tavern. "Well, that settles it. You guys get the provisions. The rest of will check out the tavern."

As Rackham and his crew headed up the mountain, the rest of us left to the tavern.

CHAPTER IX

THE HAUNTED CAVE—RACKHAM'S BIT

The three of us carried the river boat up to the mountain through a path that the pirates must have left. Since it was the exit I assume there was no reason to scare off trespassers. I understood Jack not really approving of Pr. Black, but I still believe in giving people the benefit of the doubt.

Of course, Gary Johnson has been my first mate for well over ten years. So I was quite confident of his integrity as a man. Even if he did drink a bit too much.

The climb up the mountain was very quiet which I was hoping it would be. I feel the more talking there is the more conflict there's bound to be. Thinking about that got me thinking about what Jack had done, his

● ● ● ●

withholding of information. I guess I would have done the same thing if I was in his position. So I can't really blame him. Still, in all honesty it didn't really make me feel too good.

The path that the roguish settlers made was a decent one. They definitely did some rock crushing to make the path.

As we got to the entrance, I had the professor go first. If there's to be any risk, I am not above sending my least favorite team member ahead. I noticed that the back entrance also had a carving atop. This time it was of two mermaids on either side of Neptune. It seemed a lot more pleasant that the jolly roger even with what we knew was inside. Ironically, that just made me feel worse.

As Pr. Black went inside I gave Johnson a worried look. He nodded as if he understood. Neither of us believed in ghosts or curses but what we were afraid of was booby traps and other such deadly things. "Think the island is haunted?" I asked him.

"No," He confirmed. "But I still believe that this is a dangerous place. We should take every precaution that we can." I nodded in agreement.

• • • •

Luckily, there was a slight pathway on side of the cave to walk on in order to beat the current. We walked on the path until the strength of the current lessened.

We put the river back in the water and rowed to the beach entrance. Pr. Black lit up a cigar. As he did that, Johnson and I turned on our flashlights. "Be careful. We don't know what traps those scallywags set up," I warned my group. Of course, Dr. Black was less cautious than I would have liked him to be.

The strangest of the vignettes was that first one that we saw on the way back to the beach. It was of three corpses each in a coffin that stood erect. It was definitely the most straightforward of the warnings. Having Johnson flashing his light on it I took a snapshot of the scene. He smiled at what he called my morbid humor. Laughs had nothing to do with it. Maybe that scene would be useful to us later on.

As we got further and further into the cave, strange voices got louder and louder. "Once ye leave the cave, stay away from it," one voice said.

"Dare not come back," said another.

"Only death awaits on this island," said an elderly voice.

Maybe there was something to ghosts after all. I wouldn't jump to any conclusions yet, but it was quite

•   •   •   •

easy to see that the other two had heard the voices as well. However, they were just as scared as I was to say anything, Perhaps thinking that they were letting the atmosphere get to their heads . . .

Finally we made it to the skeleton at the helm. It seemed strange. The skull on the body seemed to turn his head as if was following our movement, like the bag of bones was trying to spy on us. I don't remember that on the way down the cave.

As we past it, we heard a noise, and so we looked back. Let me tell you, what we saw next erased any doubts we may have had about ghosts and other such things!

The skeleton at the helm popped out of his position, picked up a saber lying beside it and headed straight towards us! This was straight out of a Ray Harryhausen movie!

Johnson and I immediately jumped out of the boat and ran for cover trying to survive, while the poor professor just stood there, staring at the zombie pirate paralyzed in his own fear.

The pirate came closer and closer to Pr. Black who was so stricken that the poor guy wet himself. The zombie pirate hacked off Pr. Black's head like it was air. His fresh blood sprayed all over the cave!

• • • •

The zombie pirate stopped right then and gazed around the room wondering where his two other victims ran off to. Johnson stepped back. He nearly tripped over cutlass. He picked the blade up quickly and stood on guard ready to defend himself. This was my chance to kill the living dead scallywag.

I pulled out my revolver and aimed for the zombie pirate's head. I was just hoping that the head shot in most zombie movies worked for a rotting skeleton also.

The swords of the two opponents clashed and hit each other for what seemed like an eternity. I stared horrified as the pirate clearly had the advantage.

I aimed carefully ignoring my fear and praying to God that the head shot worked on these kinds of zombies.

I fired!

Bam! The head blew off in a cloud of dust as the bones of its body fell to ground. I wiped my head in relief as I sat on rock. I looked up at Johnson with worry in my eyes. "You okay?" I asked.

He looked at me for a minute before finally giving me an answer. "Yeah Eddie," he said. "Just a bit shaken up." He dropped the cutlass and grabbed a seat on a nearby rock. "I never expected something crazy like that to ever happen."

● ● ● ●

"Yeah," I said. "I know what you mean. Looks like the professor wasn't very careful though." We both laughed at that statement. "Come on, Johnson. Let's go get those provisions."

We headed out back to the beach real fast. I really felt the need for some affection from Mrs. Rackham.

And that's exactly what we did, rowing to get to the *Sea Angel*.

CHAPTER X

SEAMAN'S GROTTO

As Rackham and his group went back up the mountain my group and I headed down to Seaman's Grotto. I wasn't really sure of what to expect other than that eerie feeling that somebody would be lurking in the shadows stalking us. So I lit up a cigarette. They always made me feel more alert.

"What do you think's in the tavern Jack?" asked Lula just as unsure as I was.

"I have no idea," I said. "I just know that this place is haunted." Mrs. Rackham nodded in a gloomy state.

"What did you see?" Lula inquired.

"A dead man," I answered.

They didn't really bother asking me any more questions. I didn't have any of the answers they were

● ● ● ●

looking for anyway. All I knew was that what I saw was indeed a dead man.

We made it to the same sign with the blood and all of us felt a cold chill run down our spine. The message of blood was no longer on the sign.

"What the hell happened?" asked Lula. Poor thing. She was starting to shake but bad.

"I don't think the blood was ever there to begin with," I stated.

"It's the spirits. They're behind all of this," explained Mrs. Rackham.

I took a drag of my cigarette and I stopped my two companions and looked them both straight in the eye. "I want both of you to keep your guard up. Don't trust anything you see with your eyes."

They nodded understanding how dangerous this situation might become. I pulled out my Beretta as I opened the door and we three walked inside.

We looked around the place. It was dank and cold. The bottles of alcohol were still full yet their outsides were covered in cobwebs.

Lula turned on her flashlight and I nodded at her in gratitude. "Let's split up. Just be careful," I told them. They nodded.

I headed towards the stairs. Once I took my first step I started hearing voices coming from upstairs. It was an old fashioned couple, probably a pirate and his wench-for-a-night. Wow. A real ghost town filled with pirates no less. This place was getting more and more exciting.

As I went further up the stairs the voices got louder and louder and louder. Once I got to the top I heard every word that was spoken. I will refrain from describing the conversation due to the explicit content of it.

I took a drag of my cigarette as I stood to the side of the door and knocked. But the voices were too busy having some fun. I knocked again and still there was no reply.

I busted open the door and it was completely empty. So I figured there wasn't any harm in scoping the place out. I opened up the drawers and they were filled with old clothes from the 1700s. They were real pirate clothes. Not just some Halloween costumes. I was pretty impressed with that find. Just these antique clothes alone could be worth a decent amount of cash.

I went to the desk and there was a quill pen with a decent amount of parchment. It looked like I wouldn't even need to find the treasure room. Not with all these antiques.

• • • •

Then my head spun towards the bed. Up above it was a map of the entire town. I smiled as I slowly removed it from the wall. I did a quick study on it and smiled at the find. This place was going to make The entire crew a big fat fortune. I hurried downstairs to show the others. I was loving this place.

Once I got downstairs I whistled for Lula. It's a whistle mainly for me and her. We got it from West Side Story.

But as I did so, there was some horrible screams! Whether it was Lula or Mrs. Rackham it was hard to tell. I was too panicky to discern the voice. All I know was that it was coming from a back room on the first floor.

As I ran to see what was going on the screams kept getting louder and louder. I kicked open the door like they do in all the action movies. Looking back at it in retrospect, it was kind if cheesy.

What I saw was something I in no way expected to see. Lula was screaming looking at the floor, My gaze followed hers expecting to see the corpse of Mrs. Rackham or a similar scenario. It turned out to nothing more than a tarantula.

• • • •

I slowly walked towards it and gently picked it up. I escorted the thing outside where I gently laid it down and started chuckling a bit.

I walked back in the room and smiled at my sister. "It's outside," I politely told her. "I have the proper anti-venom in my satchel anyway."

"I hate spiders, Jack," she told me as she ran towards me. I embraced her like any loving brother should.

"It's alright, Sis. It'll be just fine," I comforted her.

I sat her gently on the bed and I gave her the hugest smile I could muster up at the time. "Well," I started. "I may have found something that might help around the island," I told her.

"What?" There was a hint of skeptical tone in her voice.

"It's a map of the island. On top of that, it has the location of the town treasury," I told her.

At the sound of that her eyes popped open wide. A big fat smirk spread across her face. "You mean the rich stuff?"

"The rich stuff."

"Gold and jewels?"

"As much as we can get our filthy hands on."

●　●　●　●

She immediately jumped up from the bed and started dancing about. I loved seeing my kid sister. She kept shouting in a sing-song manner, "We're gonna be rich! We're gonna be rich!"

I lit myself up one of my Morley's and I looked her straight in the eye and said, "Damn straight, we're gonna be rich."

Just then Mrs. Rackham entered the room. She seemed scared and depressed. By themselves, those are some terrible feelings. Together there is no other worse feeling.

I took a drag of my cigarette and asked what was wrong.

All that she could say at that moment was, "We should leave."

CHAPTER XI

READING BONES

I asked Mrs. Rackham what she saw as she gazed at the floor weeping in fear. I very gently grabbed her shoulders with great concern. "Mrs. Rackham, you have to tell what you saw," I told her.

"I read some bones," she explained sobbing on my shoulder.

Reading bones is an old African custom brought to New Orleans. It consists of saying a chant and dropping the bones on a flat surface. However they land tells you a little bit about your future.

"The penny drops," I said getting up. "Pray tell, what did the bones say?" I inquired.

"That we're all as good as dead," she said weeping into her cupped hands.

• • • •

I turned to Lula who was just confused. "What? Somebody carved a threat on a pile of bones?"

"No, no," I told her. "It's like reading tea leaves. It's a fortune telling thing. A message carved on bones. Who are we? Temperance Brennan and her crew?" I joked.

It was as if a light bulb went on inside her head. She could pretty absent-minded that. "Oh, okay."

"How long have you been reading bones?" I asked Mrs. Rackham.

"About two years," she explained. "Eddie was going on all these voyages and I wanted make sure that he'd come back to me safe and sound."

"Have you ever gotten an ill fortune before coming to Moon Island?"

"Yes," she said. "I have."

"Were you able to change said ill fate?" I asked with a smile.

She started smiling. She rose from her seat. "Yes, I have been able to change ill fate before. It's not set in stone as God's will is."

Southern folk are quite religious, even the ones who practice such hoodoo rituals.

"Then Mrs. Rackham, let's change fate," I said. She ended up dancing around in glee with Lula. "By hook or crook, let's change our fate." I lit up a cigarette for Lula as Mrs. Rackham smiled at my suggestion.

Chapter XII

REGROUPING

I waited outside the tavern for the others having a smoke. That ride up the river cave was a good half hour by boat.

It was about an hour and a half before the others had showed up. Of course, it was blatantly that obvious there were only two who had returned while three had originally left.

"Where's Pr. Black?" I asked. Something was up and I wanted to know what.

Rackham looked me with a devil's eye. He was not happy about the answer he had to give. "Pr. Black is dead. His head was hacked off."

"How?" I demanded.

•　•　•　•

Johnson answered. "You wouldn't believe us anyway."

"Did one of the ghosts get him?"

"Yes, Sir. It was a ghost. But it was not like any ghost that I have ever laid my poor boy eyes upon," answered Rackham.

"Then please tell me so we can figure this out, Rackham," I pleaded. As much as I loved the idea of fortune, the safety of my team will always come first.

"Remember the skeleton at the helm?" he asked. I nodded. "Somehow that thing came to life attacking us. Johnson and I ran for cover. But Pr. Black? He couldn't move. He just stood there freaked out. That thing came after him."

"Well," I said, "I think it's safe to say that this island is without a doubt haunted." Johnson and Rackham looked at each other with great worry.

We walked inside the tavern. Lula and Mrs. Rackham were sitting at a table chatting up a storm. But once she saw her husband safe and sound, she ran from her chair and gave him the biggest hug that she could muster up. The poor thing balled on her husband's shoulder.

"I was so worried about you, Eddie," she said softly.

Unable to gather up any anger he asked, "You've been reading them again?" She nodded. And all he could do was embrace his wife.

Concerned, Lula questioned the whereabouts of Pr. Black.

"He's dead," Johnson told her.

I took a drag of my cigarette. I had everybody sit down at a table as did I.

"While you and Johnson were out, Rackham, your wife, my sister and I agreed that this island is in fact haunted," I started. "I don't know about you two but I'm starting to believe in ghosts."

"Then shouldn't we get the hell out of here?" questioned Rackham. "I mean we have no idea what we're up against."

"Well," I pondered, "We should leave only if the risk is greater than the prize."

"What are you suggesting, Jack?" asked Johnson with a bit of curiosity in his voice.

"The stuff in this tavern alone is enough for all of our paychecks," I said. "The parchment in the rooms, the clothing and bed sheets? Those are antiques!"

Rackham spoke up. "Then let's get the stuff out of here and head back to New Orleans."

● ● ● ●

"Not so fast there," I halted him. "That's just this tavern. What about the other places in the town? Not to mention the treasury."

"What treasury?" asked Johnson, his eyes bulging like Rat Fink's.

"Why, the town treasury, Johnson," I told him with the all the qualities of Mephistopheles. "Think about it. You'll be as rich as a king!"

Mrs. Rackham looked down to floor sorrowfully, unsure of the whole situation. "I don't know, Jack. These ghosts? They raise too many damned questions. And if the only way to change fate is to leave than that's what I would like to do."

I pondered that little speech for a moment not quite sure what to do. I didn't want to let go of this chance, but I didn't want to disregard Mrs. Rackham's wishes either. Then I had it. "Then I want you and your husband to stay right off shore while the rest of us go through with this."

"We don't need anything from the treasury either," Rackham told us. "So don't worry about us." Mrs. Rackham nodded at this suggestion.

This didn't sit too well with me. If they hadn't decided to head our crew there wouldn't be any voyage.

• • • •

To leave them out would be disrespectful towards the Rackhams.

"That I cannot do," I told them. "You two have been a major part of the voyage. To do so would be an act of disrespect."

"All we did was cook and drive," countered Mrs. Rackham. "We didn't really do anything for you guys, Jack."

"Driving and cooking? In and of themselves that's a much bigger risk than other people would take," I told her. "To top it all off, your husband dealt with my withholding of information with such dignity that I would feel insulted if you didn't take your share of the rich stuff."

Mrs. Rackham pondered my gratitude for a moment. She reached into her purse and pulled out a small cloth bag. She muttered something in French and dumped the contents of the bag on the table. They were her bag of bones. She looked at the bones then at her husband. They talked real quietly in a Cajun dialect for a few moments.

"We'll stay onshore with you guys," Mrs. Rackham told us. "If you hold us in such high regards if would be disrespectful to you to go offshore."

•   •   •   •

At the sound of this suggestion I became both curious and concerned. Was it my place to refuse them? Or should I let them accompany us? I had to ask. "What did the bones say Mrs. Rackham?"

"The best way I can describe it in English is 'damned if we do, damned if we don't,'" she told us. She motioned me over implying she wanted a cigarette.

"I thought you didn't smoke," I mentioned.

"I don't smoke, but I did," she explained.

I walked up to her and I handed her cigarette. I lit it up for her. She thanked me with one of her smiles.

"Are you really up this?" I asked, not quite sure what to make of their change of hearts.

After taking a drag of her cigarette, she handed it to her husband who took a puff. "You scratch our back, and we'll scratch yours," said Eddie Rackham.

"Good choice," I told them. "So what's our plan of action then?" If there's thing I've learned in all my experiences it's never question anybody once they agree with you. They can always change their mind.

"It is getting pretty late," said Lula. "And I'm starting to get hungry. I suggest we set ourselves up for the night and head to the treasury bright and early tomorrow."

• • • •

"I rather get it out of the way and then crash here," said Johnson not too thrilled with my sister's suggestion.

"Here's the problem with that," I told him. "Once we get whatever is inside the treasury, those ghosts are going to come after us tooth and nail. Without going to the treasury just yet, the risks of the ghosts coming after us is less."

Rackham thought on this for a second and then he looked at Johnson. "I agree with Jack on this."

"So do I," said Rackham.

Taking it rather well Johnson gave us a simple,

"Okay."

CHAPTER XIII

THE PARLAY

The dinner that Mrs. Rackham had whipped up was quite delicious; the best muffulettas that I ever had. A muffuletta is a type of sandwich made with an olive salad. The sandwich was to definitely superb.

The conversation was cordial enough. It was mainly about the music indigenous to New Orleans, or at least the South. All in all it was a quiet evening.

For some strange reason though, there was a sense of mistrust I guess you'd call it. It was especially clear towards Johnson. It kind of broke my heart to think about it; everybody was paranoid about each other. I mean the treasury was supposed to be promising.

• • • •

That night, however, was an entirely different story . . .

Everybody went to bed pretty early. I would say about ten o'clock. I, of course, decided to stick with the room that had the map of the town hanging on the wall. Maybe I would get to calculate some decent paths to the treasury. As it turned out, it was ultimately a good choice because I got a surprise that night.

As everybody else headed off for bed I lit myself a cigarette and smoked it right outside the window so the smell wouldn't consume the room. My mind was going 90 miles an hour with both fear and excitement not knowing what to expect for the next day. Was gold and jewels beyond any of our wildest dreams waiting for us, or a certain horrible death?

I went to take a look at the hanging map so I can have a decent idea of where we would be going. I was pleasantly surprised. The town was a bit bigger than I expected it to be.

Suddenly, I heard a clicking sound. Slowly drawing my firearm I turned my torso around. What do you know? It was Israel Adams aiming a flintlock pistol right between my eyes.

"Hand me the map mate," he said to me.

"Or what? You're gonna kill me?" I sneered.

• • • •

"Ay, that I will," he informed me.

"Are you a good shot?" I asked.

"Not that I require it with you so close, but I be damn good," he boasted.

"Well Mr. Hands, I'm better than Joseph Flint and I have you right in my sight," I warned him. "So I highly suggest you give me a parlay with your captain whoever it might be."

He burst out in mocking laughter. "You're going to kill a ghost?"

I lowered my aim towards his shoulder and I damn well fired my gun. Blood gushed out for a brief second. He looked shocked at the idea. "Legend has it that rock salt can do some major damage to ghosts."

"What be your request?" he asked looking down to the wooden floor.

"Who's your current captain?" I inquired.

"Jack Moonscar," he said.

"But didn't his crew have a mutiny?" I asked.

"Wasn't that before the Spanish ambushed him here?"

"It was he who led the mutiny," he said. "The Captain was indeed Benjamin Jukes."

The name rang a bell. So why couldn't I put my finger on it. I said the name to myself a few times before finally remembering.

"When did Moonscar become the Captain of the *Lady Doom*?" I asked.

"Right before Jukes killed us," he explained.

I thought about it for a moment. All the tales about Captain Moonscar were really about Jukes. "Who survived the massacre of the crew? Who hid?"

"Remy De Chagney was his name," he said.

"I wish to speak to Moonscar," I told the ghost.

"And what if I refuse?"

I smiled with authority. "Now I'm sure that your dear old Captain would consider it bad form not to accept a parlay, Mr. Adams."

Israel pondered that statement for a moment then he gave me a dirty look. "If you would, please follow me."

I start to follow Israel when he stopped me and he looked sternly into my eyes. "Leave the pistol here, Mate," he told me.

I gave him a scornful little laugh. "You and your crew Mr. Adams are pirates. By definition alone you are an untrustworthy lot," I explained. "So if you want me to leave it, you're going to have to kill me."

• • • •

He gave me a wry smile, knowing I wasn't some stupid idiot. "Right, then. Let's be off."

As we walked around the town, my mind was once again racing. Remy de Chagney must have had a lot of respect towards Moonscar and none whatsoever regarding Benjamin Jukes if he was willing to credit Moonscar with all of Juke's stories.

With de Chagney sneaking onboard the Spanish Naval ship, he must have been the one in his stories to give up the life of piracy and lead an honest life after he arrived in New Orleans. After all, the name does fit.

Either way, the key to the whole haunting seemed to be down in the bayous of Louisiana.

"Tell me a little bit about Remy de Chagney," I asked Israel. Maybe he was willing to dish out some information.

"A good man he was. He was just the cook though," explained Israel. "He wasn't really a pirate. Never did he join in us in our pillaging and plundering. He was a bit of an accomplice he was."

"How clean were his hands?"

"It wasn't until after Moonscar had formed camaraderie with him that Remy began to change," he told me. "Even then, he was quite smart, he was."

• • • •

There's no doubt that Jukes didn't take the mutiny all that well. Overcome with a hellish rage he had massacred his own crew. The Spanish soldiers who ambushed the crew didn't help any. Of course, de Chagney had escaped. I assume it was as a stow away. The real story behind this haunted pirate island was becoming quite clear dear old Jackie Boy. I may not even need the Feds' help.

Finally we had made it to a dark stone fortress on the other side of the island. What seemed like torches made of bone had lit our pathway. Fearsome, blood-thirsty cutthroats guarded our path through the gloomy fortress of dungeons. Of course, as Israel first appeared, the pirate guards were able to fake with ease a corporeal form.

I looked through one of the barred openings and I saw two long since decomposed pirate corpses stuck in a game of chess for all eternity. The game was such a stale game.

We walked up some stairs through a double door. Inside the doors was what I would like to call a pirate's court.

It was a place fit for a roguish king. It had the most extraordinary British tapestries and quite elegant

• • • •

furniture. But even then, the usual wear-and-tear of a haunted place had caught up with this place.

Cobwebs and nasty cracks filled the court up. Blood splashes made a terrible decoration.

All these sea rogues sat at tables with their bonny sea wenches, giving them some real tender, loving affection. Perhaps it was a little bit too much affection.

Israel and I had walked to the pirate sitting on his throne. He was dressed handsomely in calico clothe. He had straight black hair and a really thin beard. He might have been handsome were it not for the nasty moon shaped scar he had so forcefully carved on his left cheek. This was Captain Jack "Moonscar" Villar himself.

And let me tell you. He didn't seem too thrilled to see old Israel. "I thought you were ordered to kill the trespassers," he said firmly.

That's when I bowed and spoke up. "I requested a parlay, Captain. I assumed that you would consider it bad form not to oblige my request."

Upon hearing this, he rubbed his chin in thought. As he did so, I noticed that a beautiful Spanish girl (who I would later learn is named Rosa) was sitting right beside the pirate captain.

• • • •

"Indeed," he said obliging my request. "Mr. Adams. That will be all." Israel gave Moonscar a theatrical bow and excused himself. In a few seconds the pirate apparition had disappeared.

Moonscar and I couldn't help but stare at each other. It was almost a curious stare although there was indeed a hint of suspicion in both of our eyes.

Finally the pirate captain spoke up. "What be your name, Sir?"

"Jack Olsen," I answered.

"And what navigates you to Isla de la Luna?" he asked me. Isla de la Luna; the island of the moon. What a pretty name for a tropical island.

"Your charts," I said with a smile. "I found them in New Orleans not too long ago, Captain."

His facial expression said to me that he was very interested in what I had to say. "Do you know who I be, Mr. Olsen?"

"You're the great Captain Jack Villar," I said in a flattering tone. "The first mate who led the glorious mutiny against Benjamin Jukes."

He was pleased with my flattery. Score one for dear old Jackie Boy. "He sided with the Spanish when his crew was ambushed, didn't he?" I inquired.

•   •   •   •

He leaned forward as curious as he was suspicious. "Yes. What of it?"

"Where I come from, Jukes was but a footnote. Your reputation is of one who is as cunning as he is ruthless," I told him. "Your reputation is that of a pirate who is to be respected." It was time to think like Michael Corleone. "Through your legend I have acquired great respect for you."

Still unsure what to make of me, Moonscar spoke. "What can I do for you?"

This was it. I hope he's as smart as Remy de Chagney. "My humble crew of adventurers is interested in the town treasury."

He laughed with mockery at the suggestion. "You really assume we would just give you the booty in the treasury do you?"

"Indeed," I said still keeping my cool. "For what purpose can the dead have with money?"

The logic of the statement hit him. "Still, we be the ones to steal it. Robbery is a form of labor. It would be bad business to do so."

"In return," I offered, "My crew will help me do everything in my power to remove the horrible curse that befell upon you."

"Freedom, says you?" I nodded. "To finally rest in peace?" I nodded. "How?'

"Does the name Remy de Chagney mean anything to you?" I asked with a devilish smile.

"What of him?" Moonscar inquired.

"He was the one who gave you your infamous legend," I answered. "He settled down in New Orleans. I believe the key to your curse is there."

Moonscar looked me over from top to bottom. He was learning that I could role with the best. "And what if I refuse your generous offer?"

I looked down to the ground. Then I looked right at

Rosa. "You have a very beautiful girl beside you. I would hate for anything bad to happen to her," I said looking right into her big brown eyes.

"She's the spitting image of dead, Sir. You know that," he said.

But right as he finished up the statement a crew member of his was blasted three time times with my rock salt filled Beretta in his heart. It was as if his entire being went through rapid decay, his skin shrinking back to bone, and then turning to dust. I aimed right as Rosa. "A little bit of rock salt goes a long way," I taunted. "Even his spirit is dead, Captain."

● ● ● ●

"You've made your point," he said. "What needs to be done?"

I looked at him with my devilish smile. "I will need to inform my crew," I said. "I will give you the confirmation by the dead man's waterfall in the morning."

"What time?" Moonscar asked.

"Wait until you hear from your Jolly Roger spy," I said.

"I wish to meet under the waterfall says I," he suggested.

"There's a tunnel under the waterfall?" I asked with surprise in my voice.

"Ay," he said. "That there be."

"Under the waterfall it is," I agreed. "Now, if you'll excuse Mr. Adams and I there are arrangements to be made."

Literally, out of nowhere Israel popped up to walk me back to the tavern. The farewells were said and we were on our way.

CHAPTER XIV

MEETING IN THE TAVERN

N ow I safely made it back to Seaman's grotto. Israel was a real help with that. He knew where all the dangerous things were.

He kept asking me about how I was going to lift the curse. He was so excited about it. He was truly miserable being damned to roam the godforsaken island for all eternity no matter how beautiful it was. I kind of felt sorry for the poor guy.

But alas, I made it to the tavern and to my room where my candle was still burning bright. I bid farewell to Israel and his disappeared once again. I blew out the candle and hopped onto the bed. It looks like it will be quite a different day than what we were originally expecting.

• • • •

But one thing troubled me. Could the curse actually be lifted or was I just bringing the scallywags a false hope?

I sat up in my bed thinking about all of the possibilities that might end up happening. What if my crew disagrees with my idea? What if we learn a little too late that the curse could never be broken? Either way, what's done is done. There's no turning back now.

With all of these worries and doubts racing around my head, I don't think that I got a single ounce of sleep that night. At least I don't remember getting any.

Finally, after what seemed like an eternity of checking my watch and looking at the window to see if daylight was near, the sun finally came out. With the giddiness of a schoolboy I hopped out of bed, and grabbed my carton of cigarettes.

I banged hard on the doors of all my crew mates. Come to think of it, I may have banged a little too hard. Johnson and Rackham both gave me real dirty looks as they opened up the door. I mustn't forget the sarcastic comments they said either. But in the name of decency I'll leave them out.

About five minutes after that, we all met in the dining room. Lula and Mrs. Rackham weren't quite up

• • • •

so Mrs. Rackham was brewing coffee the old fashioned way. That was quite interesting to see.

I lit up a cigarette and I looked around at my crew. My tone was lower by this point. "How did everybody sleep?" I asked.

All four of them implied that they had slept rather well.

"That's good," I told them. "Because I feel like I didn't get an ounce."

"Why not, Jackie Boy?" asked Lula.

"Because," I explained, "I received a visit from a ghost."

Lula was horrified while the others looked at each other with great worry in their eyes. "Oh my god," spoke Lula with intense fear in her eyes. "Are you alright?"

"Remember the hand cannons I made sure to pack for everybody?" I asked her. She nodded. "Well, they really came in handy for getting a parlay."

"A parlay?" asked a skeptical Rackham. "You got a parlay with a goddamned ghost?"

"Yeah," I said. "And it looks like our plans have changed a bit."

"How so?" asked Johnson.

"Well, the ghosts won't put up any resistance when we raid the treasury," I said. Johnson's eyes bulged out

• • • •

wide while Lula sat there with a dreamy look in her eyes. The Rackhams nodded approvingly at this new information.

"If," I added, "We go back to New Orleans first and break the curse."

That got quite the opposite reaction. Lula became the sarcastic, monotone pessimist I told you readers about before. Johnson and Rackham were throwing a fit while poor Mrs. Rackham gave me a look of extreme disappointment. That was the hardest the one to see, because there was a weak smile that said to me *it's okay*.

I hushed Rackham and Johnson before speaking up.

"Here's the deal," I said. "That guarantees safety from ghosts. They won't touch us when we come back. I rather keep my crew than go after the stupid treasure if it means any of you guys are dead."

"I want some of that rich stuff, Jackie. Please," begged Johnson. It was sad to him see him pleading like a dog.

"I think it would be safer to break the curse first," I countered.

Rackham thought about the statement I made for a moment. Then he spoke up. "What makes you think

• • • •

that the key to the curse is all the way back in New Orleans?" he asked me.

I then turned to Lula. "Sis?"

She gave me a very disinterested look then spoke with some attitude. "What?"

"What do you remember about Moonscar?" I asked with a smile.

Thinking as if it hurt, she spoke up as if it was irritating. "He was ambushed here. That's it."

"When did his career as a pirate captain begin?" asked Mrs. Rackham. I turned to Lula because I knew she had the answer.

She gave me a dirty look for volunteering her then she thought about the answer. "For a year before the Spanish ambushed him," she said. Then she turned to me making sure it's right. I nodded approvingly.

"That's how the legend goes," I told everyone. "Some people say he died in the ambush and others say he died before he was taken to New Orleans. At the time, Louisiana was a Spanish colony."

"Do you know what really happened?" asked Mrs. Rackham.

I hesitated before speaking. "As it turns out," I started, "Moonscar never left the island but his career

● ● ● ●

as a pirate captain was never official. He sailed under a Jolly Roger but he was not a captain."

Of course, Lula was indeed quite blown away by this revelation. "Then how did the legend we know spread?"

"A Cajun by the name of Remy de Chagney escaped the ambush," I told everyone. "It's safe to assume that he snuck aboard the Spanish ship as a stowaway, where pirate captain Benjamin Jukes was held prisoner."

Lula was smart. She put all of the pieces I gave her together. "The stowaway credited Moonscar for what that other captain did."

"Bingo," I said.

"But that still doesn't explain why you think that the key to the pirate curse is all the way back in New Orleans," countered Rackham.

"It's safe to assume that when de Chagney made his escape," I said, "That he took something that shouldn't have been taken from the island."

Rackham looked at me suspiciously. "And why exactly is it safe to assume that?"

Even though I knew in my heart of hearts that the answer to this haunting was back in Louisiana, I had no solid proof. I gave it my best shot. "Please," I said. "Trust me on this."

Rackham shook his head in disagreement. "I can't, Jack. I need something solid," he said.

Upon hearing this doubt, I looked at everyone else in the room. It was quite clear to my saddened heart that I was not going to win this battle. Even Lula didn't care about New Orleans. I looked down and then back up at everyone.

"We have another parlay," I told them. "We meet under the waterfall."

"What does that give us?" asked Johnson.

"It gives us an opportunity to do some more bargaining with the ghosts," I explained.

"When?" asked Mrs. Rackham.

"Ghosts have a funny way of knowing where you're at if you're on their island," I said with a smile. The whole crew gave a little chuckle at this statement. At least the mood wasn't totally killed. "Shall we head off?" I asked.

They all agreed and we headed for the tunnel under the waterfall, rock salt firearms in hand. Of course, only I knew that the guns had rock salt instead of lead inside of them. I smiled for I was the only one who knew that we were safer than we thought.

CHAPTER XV

WHEELIN' 'N' DEALIN'

A s we walked to the waterfall, all of us felt a chill running down our spines. It wasn't because of the weather. That was already burning hot. I guess it had more to do with the unknown. After all, whether they're alive or dead they are still murderous rogues.

The light rain that was coming down didn't really help much either. Even if the rain is a tropical rain it still gives off a disquieting aura of gloom and doom. This was one morning where I would smoke like a chimney. Kids don't start.

Finally we made it to where we left the boat. Lula looked worried. Even Rackham wasn't too sure how to handle this situation. Maybe the ghosts aren't even real. But if that were the case what the hell happened to the professor?

We were all having a bad case of apprehension as we got on the boat and headed for the waterfall.

Needless to say going through the waterfall got us soaked almost beyond reason, but I digress.

Right before we went through the waterfall, I looked up to the main cave with some binoculars of mine. I could see clearly King Triton on the headpiece wink at me, confirming the time for our little meeting with the vicious Captain Moonscar.

And once we were inside, we were all grateful that we brought along some waterproof flashlights on the trip. Otherwise we wouldn't have been able to see a damned thing in that tunnel.

The further we went along in that dreadful tunnel, the stronger our apprehension grew.

We arrived at this passageway and we went in. There was an enormous cache with all these tiny islands spread out. On these islands were massive amounts of stolen jewels and gold nuggets. Pearls and golden statuettes filled the islands. It was mesmerizing; a treasure hunter's dream-come-true. Especially Johnson's eyes were spotting the gold with a dopey greed.

• • • •

On the largest island stood Moonscar, Rosa and few members of his criminal crew including Israel Adams. They were dressed in a more raggedy variation of what I saw them wear last night. They must have one dress code for work, and an entirely different one for pleasure.

My crew sailed up to that island and I alone had gotten off the boat and walked over towards the pirate ghost captain, unsure of how this would turn out.

"What say you?" asked Moonscar.

"I've come to further negotiate our deal Captain," I told him.

"Is your crew in accord with my salty old crew?" asked Moonscar.

"Before I answer that," I said. "I would like to be reminded of what we had previously agreed on exactly."

"That your crew would travel to New Orleans, break the curse and then come back for the gold in the town treasury," spoke Moonscar a bit taken back by the request.

I shook my head in disagreement and stared at him.

"What? Is that not what we had previously agreed upon?" he inquired.

• • • •

"Captain?" I addressed him with some authority. "We had never agreed upon which order the arrangements would be carried out."

"You mean you want to take the treasure before you take the curse?" asked Moonscar trying to clarify what I was saying. I nodded.

Once I did so, his crew laughed in belittlement. Of course, I didn't really appreciate it but I could understand their lack of trust.

"I can't do that," he exclaimed. "None of my crew knows yours. How could we trust them blokes?"

"We are honest sailors," I said. "Our word is *my* bond."

"I'm a pirate," he explained. "I don't trust a soul except me."

"Please," I begged. "Is there anyway to accommodate my crew?"

"No," he said. "I have other matters to attend to."

This was becoming ridiculous. "What the hell do you mean 'other matters'?" I asked with great defiance. "You guys are dead! How can you have anything to do?"

Moonscar smiled at me sardonically. "My dear sir," he said, "Has it ever occurred to you that me crew just might not have any interest in your proposal?"

"So what are you saying, Captain?" I wondered.

•   •   •   •

"I be saying that your crew is no friend of Lady Luck," he said chuckling.

There are three ways about this that I could go. One would be the rage and fury that these bloodthirsty bastards are used to. That will get my crew killed in seconds. This isn't *Raiders of the Lost Ark.*

The second way I could deal with this situation is to give up peacefully. And let them win. That would ultimately piss off my crew and they'll get themselves killed while they attempt a raid. That was just as ridiculous.

The third way I could go about the situation is perhaps the cruelest, yet the most cunning. It's called the fake-out. I gave a weak smile.

"Well," I said. "I hope that this doesn't interfere with what we originally agreed upon. May my crew join you for dinner this evening so we have a send-off party perhaps?"

Moonscar was excited about the idea. Hopefully he will overestimate the value of my politeness and view it as a sign of weakness.

"Do you recall your way to our courtyard?" he asked seemingly taking the bait.

"Yes I do," I confirmed.

• • • •

"Very well," he answered. "How about at dusk? What say you, Jack?"

I thought about it a moment. Does that give me enough time to do what I needed to do? It would have to do if I'm ever going to make this work. If I'm ever going to make this convincing then I had to appear weak to Moonscar.

I looked Moonscar straight in the eye with the most misleading smile I could show him. "That would be wonderful," I said. I held out my hand for him to shake which he did with such willingness.

He turned to his pillaging crew of black hearted sea dogs. "Mates!" he shouted with glee. "This vicious curse will be broken by the word of this man!" he pointed towards me with his ghostly cutlass and his crew went wild with excitement and the anticipation of finally resting in peace.

I smiled and cheered with them not fully realizing how ruthless I was becoming at that moment. One way or another, we were going to take raid that treasury before returning to New Orleans.

I turned to that scar-faced ghostly sea rogue with brilliantly false gratitude. Even I was unable to see any lies in my actions. "Captain?"

He turned to me with a smile.

• • • •

"Ay?" he asked. "What can I do for you?" he was completely unaware of what was in my head.

"I want to thank you for the hospitality your crew is showing mine," I said. "It really does make us feel welcome here on Isla de la Luna."

He smiled at me holding his right arm in the air as flamboyantly as Little Richard. "My dear Sir!" he half shouted at me with joy. "Be merry for this a joyous time! We'll be rid of this horrid curse while your crew will become rich beyond your wildest dreams!" I smiled at him for his compliment.

I then turned to face Lula and the others. They looked like they were ready to commit mutiny themselves so I slipped them one of my coldest smiles. That got them curious.

CHAPTER XVI

DEATHLY PLANNING

I truly was becoming ruthless. As my crew and I left the cache, I could tell they were noticing a change of me. Perhaps I was becoming a bit of a pirate, for I myself was feeling colder and deadlier than I ever have before that moment when I faked my sincerity with Moonscar.

Johnson seemed to gain a greater respect. Poor Rackham, he was just a bit confused at the deadlier change in me. Mrs. Rackham was concerned about my coldness.

The only thing that gave me even a hint of remorse was my sister. It seemed when she looked at me there was a fear in her eyes. Lula was scared of her own brother.

● ● ● ●

We got out of the tunnel and we all walked back to the tavern. I looked over at Lula. The poor thing was shivering and it wasn't because of the water either.

She was just plain terrified . . . of me . . .

We entered Seaman's Grotto and everybody sat down.

Then I spoke. "I know that all of you have noticed a change in me since the meeting with Moonscar."

"I have never seen such a rapid change in a single soul," exclaimed Mrs. Rackham.

"Well," I said, "It looks like I have a bit of a devil in me."

She smiled at the irony. She was starting to sort of appreciate it.

"While we're at the dinner with Moonscar, I want all three of you to do some ghost killing," I told them. "It doesn't really matter on a moral level if you kill a ghost because they are already dead."

After pondering this new thought, they seemed to be a little more at ease than when this conversation first started.

"I guess I never really thought about it that way," said a pleasantly surprised Rackham.

• • • •

"Now once we're at the dinner I will decide who you will all kill," I told them. "Did any of you notice the red head that was hanging around Moonscar?"

They all nodded. Johnson was giving a lecherous smile as he heard that. "Damn, she was gorgeous. I wish I could get her into bed."

"Good," I said. "You're gonna be the one to kill her."

Upon hearing that, Johnson froze. "Why me?" he asked uncomfortable with the assignment. "Why wouldn't you be able to kill her Jackie Boy?" The poor guy was sweating. "I mean I can do a no-name creep, but that's Moonscar's girl."

"I can't commit any of the kills," I said. "I need to be present for the duration of the party. Moonscar can't expect anything."

Mrs. Rackham gave a little chuckle. "Why, Jackie! You're becoming an organized criminal."

I smiled. "I'm actually basing a lot of this on there." They all laughed and I put my hand up to hush them. "If we show them pirate jerk offs that we mean business, you better believe that they'll give us what we want and when we want it."

"So we do that by getting organized?" asked an unconvinced Rackham. I nodded. "We wipe out three

● ● ● ●

major players and that alone is going to make them pirates take us seriously?"

For a moment, I thought about how to answer the question. Then it came to me. "If this was 1920s Chicago and you were Al Capone, would you take me seriously if I killed three of your major players just so you could listen to what I have to say?"

Rackham didn't have to think about that one. He nodded with discomfort. He was catching on that I was playing as hardcore as Moonscar, just in a more cloak in dagger style.

"You're really going to kill ghosts? How the hell can you?" asked Lula. She was looking at us like we were idiots.

"What do you mean 'how can you'?" I asked a bit confused.

"You make it sound like it's so easy," she said.

"They're already dead. They have been for over 200 years."

"Well," I said. "Once you put it that way it does sound impossible. But then again, I have heard that rock salt does the trick, Lula. I tried it out and it does work." I explained her.

● ● ● ●

After hearing me put it that way she pondered it for a moment. Then she gave me a devilish smile. "It does sound cruel. I like it, Jack."

Once again I took the floor. "Do you all know what you're going to do?" I asked. I didn't want the slightest of slip ups. They had all nodded. "Good. Now show me that when we go out there and kill the bastards." They all smiled at the thought.

I went to my room to see if I had any cigarettes left. Low and behold, I did. I lit one up. Ah, that felt better. My mind didn't at all feel so cluttered any more. Maybe I could think more clearly. Nicotine, after all, is a stimulant.

CHAPTER XV

DINING WITH PIRATES

W e headed out to the court. It was almost as if we were going in slow motion showing the pirates how damned cool we were.

It was a fairly easy to the court yet we all kept quiet. If it was a fearful silence or an excited silence, I don't know. I assume both. But that's way it was.

As we arrived, two pirates tried to stop us until old Israel Adams arrived. "Let them in," he said. "The Captain's orders." The guard did so.

I nodded at Israel in gratitude. I liked him. He was going to be safe. He led through those horrible dungeons. I didn't feel any less frightened than I did the first time around. I looked at my crew and they were just as uncomfortable with the grim scenario as I was.

● ● ● ●

"Is the Captain available at the moment?" I asked.

"Yes," he nodded. "He'll be right down, he will." His smile was a truthful sincerity. I couldn't help but admire him.

"Good, because I am downright starving!" I said with a quirky politeness. Everybody laughed while I pretended to. To this day I can't believe that I said something that corny.

As I said that corny line, however, Moonscar had materialized right in front of my eyes. And I must say even with that nasty disfigurement on his face he looked handsome. I have to admit that rogue had some real style.

"How do you, Captain?" I asked waving my hand at him.

"I'm doing well, Lad. Just well," he said with a festive smile on his scarred face. "How do you do this evening?"

I smiled along with him. "I am honored to be here Captain," I said. I wanted to make sure my flattery would get me somewhere. "This is a lovely court you pirates have."

"Why thank you," said Moonscar. "Even in death we make attempts at cleanliness."

● ● ● ●

"Your attempts are well appreciated, Captain." So far I was indeed winning him with compliments. I bowed.

As I did so, I saw a gorgeous sight. From the back of the room a girl dressed in the most elegant of red dresses started slowly to walk forward to my crew and Moonscar. As she got closer, I saw that it was the red head that had me starring.

I glanced around and noticed that I wasn't the only one that was completely drunk in admiration. Every other male in court was. Especially Johnson. This was perfect.

Finally she made to us and she immediately took the arm of Moonscar. The wench had laid her head on the pirate's shoulder. "Aren't you going introduce me to your amigos?"

"I am sorry," he said. "This be Jack Olsen. He's going to break this curse. Jack, this be Rosa de la

Rojos."

She held out her hand to me palm down and I grabbed it to kiss it. "It's a pleasure, Senorita." I said.

As she gave me a slight smile, I know that she'd be putty in Johnson's hands. Even though he can be a real pervert he is even more so quite the gentleman. I was

• • • •

certain that Moonscar was nowhere the status of a true gentleman.

"The pleasure is all mine, Senor," she told me with such a gorgeous Spanish smile.

"Let me introduce you to my comrade," I told her. "His name is Tom Johnson. I think you two would get along just fine."

I waved over to Johnson and he came as if he was a loyal dog. "Mr. Johnson? I would like you to meet Rosa de la Rojo," I told him. "I would like you two to get to know each other."

It has become Johnson's job.

Chapter XVI

JOHNSON'S HIT

I was introduced to the Spanish ghost by Jack She was absolutely stunning with fiery red hair, and her gorgeous Spanish dress. I couldn't help but fall for her right away. "How do you do?" I asked as I took her hand to kiss it.

She smiled at me. "Muy bueno," she said with great interest in me. "Especially with such charmers as Senor Olsen and . . . you."

The way she hesitated on the word *you*. I became enchanted with her. I was unsure I would be able to go through with the job.

"What about the Captain?" I asked innocently as if I didn't want to become between them.

• • • •

"Moonscar thinks of me as no more than a whore," she retorted. "I would hardly say I have any kind of romantic relationship with him. He is not good enough for me to allow him to call me 'novia'."

This is getting good. "How so?" I asked. I was hanging on every word she was saying.

"He has no manners. He doesn't know how to treat a lady," she explained. "Especially a dignified Spanish lady such as myself."

"I'm sure he doesn't know any better," I tried to console her. As always it didn't work. It never works for me to begin with.

"Ay, he is just a dirty carbon," she said. She was getting a bit flustered.

"Would you like to take a walk with me?" I asked holding out my elbow.

She smiled at with her luscious red lips as she took my arm. "Si," she said. "I would love to, Senor Johnson."

I smiled at her as if I was allowing myself to fall for such a treasure. But even then, I knew what had to be done was going to get done no matter what. That being the case, I was starting to feel a little sick. It didn't matter if she was already dead.

● ● ● ●

We walked around the outside of the court. It was an ugly place filled with cracks and cobwebs. There was a sense of apathy coming from the place. I was starting to get the feeling that nothing was as it seemed in this hellhole, perhaps not even Rosa.

But the weird thing was that I was really enjoying our conversation. It seemed natural.

"How long have you been dead?" I asked with a genuine curiosity in me.

"About 270 years," she said solemnly. "I can't recall exactly it doesn't matter any way. I'm just Una del muerta." One of the dead. As she spoke this saw the irony of the situation.

"Why don't you enjoy your death like you enjoyed your life?" I asked her.

"Because these men are evil!" she snapped. "Even in death all they care about is fulfilling their selfish deeds. I hate them all. I hope that once the curse is lifted they all rot in Hell."

"Some passionate words," I said a just little taken back by the words. It was a little deeper than what I really had desired to go.

"Why did you bring the gun?" she asked.

What could I say? The only thing that I felt like I could say was "How did you know?"

• • • •

"Come one," she said. "I'm not stupid like any of these drunkards, Johnson."

"I came here for an assassination," I said looking at the ground in guilt.

"It has rock salt. Si?" I nodded. "Who are you going to kill?"

Damn it! Why did it have to be that question? Why couldn't it any other question?

"Who? Me?" She was starting to get loud by now.

"Moonscar," I said.

"Don't be chicken. Talk," she said with the utmost sincerity.

I had gotten a little flustered by then. I looked her straight in the eye. "And if it was you, Rosa? What then?"

A single tear started falling from her eye. And then a wry smile appeared on her face. I was confused. It was partly with her, with the fact that I was falling for her when she was not only a stiff but also my victim.

"What the hell are you smiling about?" I asked a little edgy. "Do you think it's funny?"

"I want you to kill me," she said as her tears became stronger on stronger. "Kill me, Johnson. I don't this cursed death any longer."

• • • •

At this suggestion. I became furious. Why? I have no idea. It should have been easier for me to kill her when I knew she wanted it but it wasn't easy at all. "Why the hell would you want me to that? Huh? I can't see any difference."

"Because," she pleaded, "I just want to rest in peace. I am miserable in this godforsaken island with all these evil men! Por favor!" As she pleaded, I couldn't bare the sight of her tears.

"Is there any other way?" I asked.

She shook her head, and then I looked down to the ground. I couldn't believe I was going to do this. "I will do anything to change this. Please, Rosa."

Damn. The first rule in assassination is don't get involved with your target. What the in the hell was I thinking?

"There is nothing else," she said.

"Get on your knees," I ordered her as I pulled out my piece. "Get down, Rosa!" I was really going to do this.

Finally she knelt and I turned to face her back. I pointed the gun at her head and t=her tears turned into sobs. As I made the sign the cross, tears flowed

• • • •

down my face. There was no turning back after this. I shot her point blank.

Her skin started to shrink into her bones. She rotted away to nothing more than that and the dress she wore. I walked back to the party with the others.

Chapter XVII

FINDING MORE HITS

J ohnson had come back to join the party with a decadently divine sense of nihilism. His face was cold and his smile was reckless. It was a wonderful sight to see.

I pulled my soldier aside. "How did it go?" I asked him.

He smiled. "I must say it went off beautifully. She was literally begging to do it."

"Wonderful," I acknowledged. "Now it's time to find a couple of pirates for the Rackhams."

I looked about and I find the Rackhams sitting in the back looking for some possibilities. I went to join them.

• • • •

"You're not interested in joining the festivities?" I asked. They looked at me and smiled. "Well, have you met any interesting pirates?"

"Well, there are a couple of possibilities," said Rackham.

"Tell me more," I said I sat down right beside them. I was starting to get excited.

"We've been watching the two sea rogues, at the entrance," said Mrs. Rackham. "There have been a couple instances where Moonscar had whispered in their ears. They saluted them."

This was where Rackham came in. "Then there are lute and mandolin players. He has talked to them also."

I pondered on this a moment. "He was most likely suggesting the next song," I said thinking aloud. Go with the ones at the entrance."

"Yes Sir, Mr. Olsen." The Rackhams were off on their deadly way. After accomplishing this task, I was all the more grateful that I was raised a loving decent home.

I went to find my sister and there she was talking to Israel Adams. I walked up to them. "Israel," I said. "I see you've met my beautiful sister."

"Ay," he said. "That I have."

"Is she to your liking?" I asked.

• • • •

"Oh she is, sir," he told me. "A real proper lady she is." He was becoming a bit bashful yet honest. I was really starting to like this guy.

I then turned to Lula. "And what about you, Sis?" I asked. "Are you taking a liking towards Mr. Adams?"

"Yes," she said with a flirtatious smile on her face. "It looks like the beginning of a beautiful relationship."

Damn. She marked him as her target. I had to stop it. "Well," I said. "What your rank, Mr. Adams?"

"I'm a boatswain," he said. What a relief. His low rank alone makes him useless as a target.

"Well make sure that friendship lasts," I told them. "I would hate to see it go to waste." As I said that, Lula seemed to get the message. She reluctantly nodded her head. "Now can I talk to you a moment, my dear sister?"

"Yes of course," said Israel as he politely backed away. "Excuse, Miss."

I got my face to her ear and whispered. "Israel is just a Pintel," I told her. "We really need to go after a Gibbs or Anna Maria. At first she looked a sort of surprised, but then a sinister smile spread across her face.

"What about that wench Moonscar has fondling for the past half hour?" she asked.

I smiled at her. "You know what?" I asked.

• • • •

"What?"

"That's absolutely perfect," I assured her. "Go get her, Kid."

I don't know. The term 'Kid' I use in veins of 'buddy' or 'dude'. I don't use it as reference to a young age.

Chapter XVIII

NIGHT STALKERS—THE RACKHAM'S HIT

T he full moon was out tonight. That was a good thing. We could still have the cover of night yet we could see our victims.

Poor Eddie. He was so unsure of this. But whether or not our victims were alive, they were evil. They had to be stopped. SO I was seeing nothing wro9ng in what we were doing.

We stood in the shadows, lurking. Of course, if a pirate walked and thanked us for helping Jack break the curse, we were still cordial.

We saw them exit towards the dungeons and we made sure to follow them. Even then, we kept our distance.

• • • •

We slowly entered into the dungeons and a cold breeze blew all round us. It was as if death was there waiting for us to do our job. I must admit, as eerie as that was it was also quite thrilling. I was getting goose bumps. We went further inside.

When we first entered the dungeons, we were a bit scared. I never really liked seeing skulls and bones everywhere. It just reminded me of death and sorrow. That was one thing I never needed reminding of.

But going through them a second time, we both felt the eerie chill of pleasure. We were excited to be performing this task.

We looked through all the barred openings so as to seem we were taking in the atmosphere. To seem morbidly curious about the tragic end of pirates. And with each set of torturous devices, we had gotten emotionally aroused as if what we were doing was exciting.

Eddie and I will be the first ones to admit that unknown to either of us; we had a real sadistic streak kept hidden inside.

Even then, we watched and waited for the just the right moment.

Finally, they stopped and talked. I pulled out a switchblade knife. Earlier in the day, I laced it with

• • • •

rock salt. I crept on over to when of the pirates as I grabbed him by the neck and slit his throat. The red strange blood of the dead gushed all over the place as his skin shrunk into his decaying bones destroying his incorporeal body. I smiled at the other raggedy rogue who pulled a Flintlock pistol on me.

Luckily that bastard didn't see Eddie coming as he pulled out his hunting knife. My wonderful hubby kept stabbing him and stabbing him as his incorporeal body went rapid decay.

I smiled at him. "Honey?" I asked. "Wasn't that fun?"

He smiled. "Killing dirty pirates is always fun, my dear." He gave me a passionate kiss. Damn. It felt so good. His luscious lips meeting mine. I was on Cloud 9.

But alas, it was time to get to the festivities. We were off.

CHAPTER XIX

I WAS A VAMP—LULA'S HIT

I saw Moonscar standing near his throne talking with Jackie Boy. It was a wonderful setup as that so-called wench was hanging all over him. Moonscar was indeed handsome. But being handsome and being sexy are two totally different things.

But I sure had my eyes on the price. I walked up to them. I wanted my fun and I was going to get it.

"Jackie Boy?" I asked my brother. "Who's this handsome devil?"

He smiled at me. "This. My dear sister, is Captain Jack Villar otherwise know as Captain Moonscar."

I held out my hand as he grabbed it to kiss it. "I am enchanted," he told me. And all I can say is that he was definitely a pirate. The man slobbered all over my hand.

• • • •

It was disgusting, but it was better than not getting into the treasury. I was more than happy to play along with him.

"You damn well should be enchanted," I told him. I will definitely be worth your while, Captain.

My brother smiled at me. "I think I'll let the two of you talk for a moment. I want to see how Mr. Hands is doing," he told us.

Moonscar was going to be putty in my hands and he didn't care. But that wench sure did. She was giving me the dirtiest of looks.

"Jack?" she said with much annoyance. "She's not lady such as I be. She is nothing more than a dirty strumpet."

I smiled a seductive smile at Moonscar. "Are you really going to let a woman control you? A dead woman might I add?" I asked.

The fury was building up in her eyes. This was just too perfect. "Why you vicious . . ."

"Vicious what?" I asked with a smile. "Vicious bitch?"

"Out of the mouths of babes!" she screamed.

"Get out of here," I said. "Nobody wants a second—rate whore around."

• • • •

As I said that her face turned red with fury. She came running at me with everything she had. The wench was falling for it. I pulled out that gun that Jackie Boy gave and I pumped four bullets into her head.

Her death was a brilliant thing to see. Everybody at the court was staring at the event in awe and fear.

Her skin was speedily sinking into the whore's bones in a grotesque display of rapid decay.

I just stood there without emotions. But I knew that this was the best way to kill; have the victim attempt to kill me. It went done beautifully. And as her bones lay there beside Moonscar and me, I turned to face him. I could see his fear. The great Captain Moonscar was afraid.

CHAPTER Xx

GETTING WHAT WE WANT

What Lula did was cheer brilliance. I couldn't have better myself. She walked over to me and smiled. I waved my hand in praise to her.

Just then, a couple of no-name pirates ran toward Moonscar from the dungeons. They looked like they had just met the devil himself.

"Captain!" one of them shouted. "Rosa has just died!"

"Rock salt?" Moonscar asked in a quiet voice. He was trying to keep his cool. They nodded.

The other one blurted out, "So are Breck and Smollett."

• • • •

His eyes became cold as he turned to me. "What be the meaning of this, Mr. Olsen?" he asked.

I pulled out my gun and I pointed the thing right at his head. I became stern. "I want access to the treasury, Captain. You're going to allow it."

His face burst into rage. He threw a goblet of wine on the ground in his fury. "Just because you kill butcher me mates?" he screamed. "Have you any idea how stupid that was? What the hell is wrong with you? Be touched by devils?"

I looked straight at him not flinching once. "Mr. Adams!" I called.

He slowly went up to me. "Yes sir?" he asked. He was so afraid, poor guy.

"You have two choices," I told him not removing my gaze from Moonscar. "You can take me to the treasury where my crew will get a share. I will then break the curse. Or you can refuse and be damned to walk this godforsaken earth for God knows how long." I said. "Now which choice will it be?"

"I will take your crew to the treasury," he said solemnly.

Just as he said that, Moonscar was burning in his anger. He was about to attack Israel but Johnson tossed

● ● ● ●

him his rock salt filled gun and good old Israel aimed it right at Moonscar.

I smiled. "You better make sure that's what you want to do, Captain."

"You vicious bastard! I'll tear your heart out!" he screamed rushing at both me and Israel.

But that pirate captain wasn't fast enough. Both me and Israel pumped that ghost wicked ghost full of lead. I took a look around. All the pirates were shocked at how his skin was melting off his face. His ectoplasmic blood was pouring all over the place.

I looked all over the court. The pirates could do nothing but stare in shock at the situation. It was quite an awkward situation.

CHAPTER XXI

THE TREASURY

I then pointed the gun at Israel. I felt my eyes grow cold as I stared right into his own eyes. "Are you going to take my crew to the treasury?" I asked him. "That's all we want."

He gave a huge grin as if he was quite pleased. "We hated him," he said. "We be taking you to the treasury as soon as you would like."

I dropped my gun and I held out my hand towards the old sea rogue. "Thank you," I told such real gratitude.

"I will definitely make damn sure that I break the horrible curse."

"Well, we never liked the bastard," he said. "We're perfectly alright as we are. He was the reason we hated this godforsaken island."

Jeff Martinez

• • • •

"Still," I said. "It would only be fair to do so, Mr. Adams. You scratch our back and we'll scratch yours."

"I think we'll like that," he said. He finally grabbed my hand and we shook on it. It turned out to be the best deal that I have every made.

I looked in his eyes and I smiled at him. "I would like to be escorted to the treasury by you, Captain Adams." I turned to face my crew. "How does that sound, guys?" They all agreed with the utmost pleasure. "Let's go."

We finally got to the treasury. It was the most wonderful experience that I ever had. The gold was from all over eighteenth century Europe as well as the ever so gorgeous Caribbean. Piles of gold filled up the room to the top.

And then I noticed something quite puzzling. It was a skeleton with a blue coat and a once shiny leather tri-corn on his head. A cutlass was jammed into his back. He was definitely more important than any of the remaining pirates.

"Who is he?" I asked Israel.

"That be Captain Benjamin Jukes," he said to us.

I turned to study the strange elegance of the skeleton. And then something quite uncanny and yet very warm happened. It looks like Benjamin Jukes was still the captain of those pirates. The skeleton of

• • • •

Captain Jukes winked at me. I smiled and winked back. And that was how I knew everything was right in Isla de la Luna.

We then took our loot as we saw fit. I still made sure to leave a decent amount of treasure for him. It would be disrespectful not to do so.

Then next day, bright and early we packed up our bags and left the island. Right before we boarded our little boat, Israel and a few of his crewmates waved. We waved back. It was now time to return the favor.

My crew was off to New Orleans to finish solving this roguish mystery. An eerie chill went up my spine as I smiled to myself and lit a cigarette. A pirate's life was definitely for me.

THE END?